# GOSSAMER & THORNS

## A GEARS OF MALEVOLENCE NOVELLA

### ELLE BEAUMONT

Midnight Tide
PUBLISHING

Gossamer & Thorns
Copyright © 2022 by Elle Beaumont

Published by Midnight Tide Publishing.
www.midnighttidepublishing.com

Edited by
BookMarten Editorial
www.bookmarteneditorial.com

*For those who love morally ambiguous characters . . . and a
stellar origin story. This one is for you.*

# ONE

"I've almost done it," Dr. Sevrein murmured. He pinched the bridge of his nose and wiped the sweat from his brow with his kerchief, which he then promptly stuffed back into his shirt pocket. Dropping his hand, he muttered and undid the buttons on his high-collared shirt. Eventually, his crystalline gaze slid to the young man at his side.

Kristoph—Kris—stood by his father and frowned, unsure of what to say. What his father was attempting to do was not only taboo, but it was blasphemous to boot. Infusing a human's soul into an automaton was playing God—but who was he to speak out against his father?

What was the point, Kris wondered, of having a human soul trapped inside a machine? They already piloted dirigibles and trains, and cleaned and tended to homes. It was only a matter of time before humans were overrun by automatons. However, Kris's father was a man obsessed with creation, especially if there were any mechanics involved.

Dr. Magnus Sevrein had inherited an earldom when his elderly father had passed, but tending to such responsibilities had never been high on his list of things to do. Instead, he hurled himself into academics and, later on, science. His younger brother, Hakon, stepped in to secure the holdings and the earldom flourished in his care.

When Kris's father married, it was to a woman who sought to climb societal ladders, and Kristoph was born some odd years later. By the grace of all that was good, he was largely raised by the nanny and ignored by his parents. Until he turned thirteen years of age.

His father had drilled into his mind the importance of a good pedigree and what it meant. Good breeding would produce better breeding—as if they were all just prized show ponies. *Good breeding means that genes are protected from Ironbark disease.* A notable disease that swept through Agderland, marking the affected ones with mismatched eyes, a weakened immune system, and inevitably a shortened lifespan. In the worst cases, the patient's body attacked itself and shut down organs, even in the youths.

It amused Kris that his father had never cared so much about legacies outside of beakers, petri dishes, and tinctures. Yet here he was, impressing the importance of smart pairings because Hakon had no son to pass the family estate to, which meant it would go to Kris.

A hiss of a curse emitted from Magnus and a fist collided with the work desk, sending a dish scattering to the floor. "Dammit." His fingers jammed through his faded blond hair. "Get out of here, I have to think. The formula for the binding liquid is off—I have to . . . " His voice trailed off and Kris knew he wouldn't finish.

Reaching into his pocket, Kris pulled out a watch and smiled down at it. It ticked away until the big hand and the little hand pointed to the twelve. In the hallway, the grandfather clock chimed, and with a grin, Kris jogged down the hall, mindful to tiptoe past his mother's room. Most days she didn't bother leaving her room. Her nerves wouldn't allow it and she took to nursing them with a good helping of belladonna. It was something he had grown used to. His parents had never been present in his life.

Quickly descending the spiral staircase, Kris made his way to the front hall and opened the door. A pair of mismatched eyes met his gaze, signifying Ironbark disease. They were the most expressive set he had ever seen: crystal-blue and amber, set in the rounded features of a pale face. Blond hair was held in a tidy chignon, but a few curls framed the doll-like face.

She wore a navy dress jacket, which had ruffles on its high neck. The cut of it tapered in toward her ribs, accentuating her slender figure, and the skirt she wore only came to her knees, allowing Kris to appreciate her legs. They weren't bare, for she wore a pair of brown tights, but he longed to do away with every speck of clothing on her. He'd respected her wishes and remained deferential, but damn if he couldn't help it when his mind wandered.

A slow smile replaced his grin as he swung the door open. "Emilie, I've been waiting for you," he crooned, waving her inside.

At nineteen years of age, Kris should've been in search of a mistress, or potentially a wife, but he'd never played by the rules. He'd certainly spent a fair amount of time entangled with young ladies, but there had always been one in particular who caused his heart to stutter and his world to slow.

Emilie.

Emilie was only seventeen and her father hadn't been keen on the idea of an engagement before eighteen. Kris could wait six months. What could possibly change in a short amount of time?

"Really?" She wrinkled her pert nose and flashed a brilliant smile at him. "I couldn't tell."

He cleared his throat, casting his eyes toward the ceiling as he feigned embarrassment. Offering his arm to her, Kris allowed her to loop hers through his. "It's been—oh, confound it—a whole four days without seeing you?" He shook his head and grinned as they walked toward the solarium.

Emilie's face lit up as they crossed the threshold. And once they were inside the room, she moved toward a table that held a single plant. She held her hands up as if she were cupping the fragile petals, but she didn't actually touch them. "How is my beautiful Pearl today?"

The Moth Orchid, as it was commonly known, less commonly known as Phalaenopsis Blume, was a vibrant hue of orange with veins of pink streaking across each silken petal. In the center a stark white was seen, and it was why Emilie named the plant Pearl.

Kris shook his head and stuck a hand in his pocket. The way she named each plant amused him, but what tickled him more was the fact that after she named it the blasted thing seemed to grow and flourish. Of course, there was a scientific reason behind it, which had little to do with a name and everything to do with carbon dioxide. Kris's father had declared that believing a name brought forth life was just hogwash. It may have been, but it warmed his heart to know Emilie loved his plants as much as he did.

"I am certain she's better now that you're here." He sighed heavily, narrowing his eyes on the plant. "She prefers your company."

"Pearl or you?" she teased him.

Moving closer to her, Kris tilted his head to catch her eye. "Me," he said, unabashedly. "I am better now that you're here." There was no point in hiding how he felt about her anymore. They were not children cast aside at a party—they were not young teens withholding laughter at an opera. They were young adults on the brink of something else, something new and exciting.

"Kris," Emilie said softly and dropped her hands, breaking the moment between them. "I have an invitation for you." She pulled her gloves free of her delicate hands and reached into her reticule. "It is six months out, so I assume you'll be able to clear your schedule."

Kris took up the invitation. Cream paper with gold lettering. Blasted thing, stealing the moment. He smiled and read it out loud. "You are cordially invited to celebrate Lady Emilie Nilsson's eighteenth birthday . . . " He paused and lowered the card only a fraction, just his eyes peering over the paper card. "You assume wrong."

Despite the glee that shone on her face, something flickered, perhaps doubt.

"I have nothing planned at all, and would be more than happy to be the first to arrive at your birthday party." He took one of her bare hands in his, felt the softness of her skin against his hands, and bowed his head to brush a kiss against her knuckles.

Emilie gasped softly, then she pulled her hand away only to remove the bonnet on her head. She watched him, color rushing into her cheeks, and Kris wished he could read her mind. "I cannot wait then. Help me tend to these beauties."

Again, Emilie navigated through the tension and pulled away. All Kris longed to do was bury his fingers in her hair, taste her lips, and proclaim his heart belonged to her . . . always.

An hour passed between entering the room and finishing their task of grooming the flowers. It was a tedious thing that the staff wasn't allowed to do, per Kris's instructions. Emilie enjoyed it, and it was fairly relaxing.

"I have a gift for you," Kris said and circled his finger to tell Emilie to spin around. "It took me a while to find it, but I think you'll be rather fond of this." He moved to the potting bench and pulled the fabric away from a covered plant. He smiled down at the strange beauty and looked to Emilie. "You may look now."

Emilie spun around and gasped as she took in the sight of the beautiful flower. It was strange looking; its petals were such a faint purple that it almost looked silver, and the dark purple veins in it made it that much more peculiar. The underside of it retained the same dark hue, giving the flower a steel-like appearance before it bloomed.

"Kris! This is . . . it's the most stunning flower I've seen," she stated softly. Without hesitation, she lifted herself on the balls of her feet and kissed the corner of his mouth.

Stunned but for a moment, Kris froze and wanted nothing more than to dip his head to turn the kiss into something more than chaste and friendly. As Emilie withdrew, a slow rakish grin tugged at his lips. "I know. I searched far and wide for one that would ensure I received a kiss."

"Kristoph Anders Sevrein," Emilie whispered, her eyes playfully narrowing as she chastised him.

Lifting his hands, he turned his attention to the plant again. "Apparently, the flower's creation was quite a task. One of the rarest hybrids out there right now."

"But, where or how did you find it?" Emilie's mismatched gaze widened.

"I have my ways." He rapped a knuckle against the pot and lifted his brows. "Take it home so that you can care for it. I have the instructions here. Along with the difficulty in creating it . . . it seems it's as finicky as the orchids." His eyes focused on her features, and he committed this moment to his memory. The soft blush painting her cheeks. Her full lips parting and begging for him to kiss them. And the sweet innocence swirling within her gaze.

A simple but weighted moment.

Outside in the hallway, the clock chimed the telltale sign of a new hour, and Magnus appeared in the doorway to the room, lifting a disinterested brow in Emilie's direction. "Your mother is requesting your presence, Kristoph. See that your guest finds her way out properly."

Kris's icy gaze flicked toward his father. It was no secret that his father thought very little of the Nilsson family and hadn't the decency to even show the tiniest bit of courtesy to them. They were beyond inferior in his eyes, for Ironbark disease ran in their family. Of course, Emilie never thought ill of Kris.

As soon as his father slid from the doorway, he

lowered his gaze. "I'm sorry," he murmured, blond hair tumbling into his eyes.

"You are not your father, Kristoph. Never forget that." She lifted a hand, brushing the strands of hair from his face. "I'll see myself out. Thank you for the gift." Emilie took a step forward and this time she brazenly pressed her lips against Kris's. "Until tomorrow."

The breath escaped Kris and he watched, dumbfounded, as Emilie walked out of the room. *Why did Mother have to ruin this moment?* Grinding his teeth, he stormed out of the room and back up the spiral staircase.

The door to his mother's room was open just a crack, and Kris wished nothing more than to flee down the hall to the privacy of his room, but alas, he had been called. He pushed inside, and the light filtered into the otherwise darkened room. His mother sat with her head propped against an array of pillows and if it hadn't been for her eyes, which were blankly staring at a spot across the room, he'd have thought her to be asleep. When Kris shifted, her eyes locked onto his.

Perhaps if he didn't move, she wouldn't see him—it was something he'd thought as a child, and sometimes it worked back then. No such luck would allow that to happen. Not as her hand swept away strands of hair from her brow, not as she scooted into a sitting position and the down blanket slid from her and revealed her ivory nightdress.

"Come sit with me, my son." She patted the bed next to her, clearly still groggy from the effects of the drug.

His feet felt weighed down as if by lead. But dutifully, Kristoph moved toward the bed and sat. "What is it, Mother?" His words were clipped.

"Can't a mother ask to visit with her son? Honestly, one would think you didn't love me at all."

He didn't. At least he was fairly certain he didn't. She had been largely absent from his life, far too busy playing hostess and occupied with staying relevant in society to pay any mind to him unless it was to parade him around like a doll. And as much as he loathed to admit it, his father had been more of an influence than she had. His mother also had a tendency to lash out and cut him down, which had hardened his heart toward her over the years.

The silence seemed to infuriate her. She curled her lip as she looked up at her son. "You act as though you are ill-bred, and we know that isn't true."

His father wasn't the only one who impressed the importance of breeding, but his darling mother wasn't strong, not like him and not like his father. She was a prisoner to the vial next to her bed and the nerves that drove her to it.

"Pardon me, but what do the ill-bred act like, Mother? You act as if they're another breed entirely." He pressed his lips into a firm line and simply waited for whatever insults she was surely about to sling his way, if she could even muster them.

"I'd prefer you find a suitable girl. Your father said that the Nilsson girl was here. You know what you'll be inheriting, so aim higher than that diseased thing." His mother and father shared the same views on strength and preserving genetics. Since Emilie was born with Ironbark, neither one of his parents viewed her as anything more than a genetic tragedy.

Red bled into Kris's vision as anger blossomed in his chest and spread throughout his body. That was enough. Insulting him was one thing, but dragging Emilie into it? He stood up and shot her a glare. "Bite your tongue, woman. Your opinion means very little to me when it comes to strength. You cannot pry yourself from bed long enough to even bathe properly, so please spare me your judgment of what strength is." He sneered and began to walk away. "We are done here."

His mother gasped as if someone had slapped her, then her gray eyes grew as cold as steel. "You will never find happiness with her, Kristoph. Never." Her lips twisted into a humorless smile, and her frame fell against the mound of pillows. She laughed tiredly, but it sounded sinister just the same and it chilled him to the core.

# Two

A loud bang, followed by the vibration of the doorjamb, startled Kris awake. His mussed hair hung in his vision, obscuring the figure standing in his doorway. But as the heavy, quick steps traveled across the floor, he knew who it was. Father.

"Get up." His father pried the down blankets from him. "Get up now. You need to help me figure this out." His voice was tight with barely restrained fury and Kris could hear the madness, too.

"What the hell time is it?" Kris croaked. A warm glow peeked through the drapes, which meant it was after seven in the morning.

Magnus Sevrein's obsession with science always drove him to madness, especially when he couldn't figure out a problem. Unfortunately for Kris, his father would drag him into it, leaving him no option but to learn the art of alchemy, when all he wanted was to study botany.

Knowing better than to argue when his father was in

such a state, Kris rolled out of bed. "Can I get dressed, at least?"

His father blinked owlishly, then, as he realized his son was in his night clothes, he nodded. "Be quick and meet me in the cellar." With the words barely off his lips, he left the room.

Quickly, Kris pulled on his trousers and a white linen button up. Over that, he wore a cerulean vest with a white paisley print on it. Once he slid his feet into his calf skin button boots, he was out the door and rushing down to the cellar, lest he deal with another tirade from his father.

The cellar was damp, as was expected, but it didn't lack lighting. It was far too bright, in Kris's opinion. Bronze gas-lamps dotted along the walls, and where there wasn't a shelf lined with bottles, gears, or some kind of tool, they cast a golden glow to the entire room. From the ceiling hung several sprawling chandeliers, each boasting a lit candle.

In the middle of it all, hung suspended by chains, a nondescript automaton stared lifelessly at the stone floor. Bronze limbs hung limp at its sides, and the smooth column of a neck tilted at the base at an unnatural angle.

It wasn't as if the machines were uncommon in Agderland, so Kris wasn't startled to see it. Several machines worked in their family home. Automatons were immortal in the sense that they were machines and couldn't die. It was far easier to replace a part than it was to replace a human. So many households employed them, and so many businesses were overrun with them too.

Kris had seen far more detailed machines before, with hair and grafted skin pulled over titanium limbs. But the quality of the machine had little to do with the success of infusing a human's soul with one and everything to do with the process and formulation. It was tedious work, but done slowly and efficiently, it was possible. Dr. Rolf Yotun had accomplished it in his last years alive. He'd even boasted of his accomplishment, hiding away his notes. But his automaton turned on him, so it was assumed, for Dr. Yotun's body was discovered outside of his home, his heart ripped from his chest. But his notes were lost when the machine set fire to his home, destroying everything, including his creation.

"Are you just going to stand there?" his father snapped, narrowing his eyes at Kris who stood at ease near the door.

"I might," Kris muttered under his breath, pushing off the wall. He crossed the room and stood at the workbench, plucking up a notebook. He pored over the text, and his eyes slanted toward the automaton then toward the silver table beside it. On the slab, a man lay shivering. "Father . . ." He froze, clutching the notebook tightly.

Kris had never killed a thing in his life and if his father thought he'd partake in extracting the man's soul, he was sadly mistaken.

His chest grew heavy as reality settled in. How had his

father gotten this man here? Pressing his lips together, Kris withheld a cry of disgust and stamped it down enough for it to be a grunt. However, his eyes grew blurry with tears of fury and revulsion.

"Don't fuss so." His father waved him off as he bent over the man. The man's sickly skin already had a gray tone to it, as if someone had drained the blood from his body. And perhaps someone had. "This is Trevor Absen. He's dying and wishes to give his body to science." His tone implied that he was doing the good man's will. Kris felt like vomiting.

Distracting himself by looking down at the notebook, Kris noted that blood had in fact been taken from the man and bound to an alchemical agent that, when pumped through the automaton, should bind and infuse the machine with the man's soul.

Blood possessed memories, which made sense. It was with a being nearly since conception. Memories were consciousness, but what of the soul? Did it run through the veins as well?

"This will ease the pain." Magnus slid a thin white tablet beneath the dying man's tongue and observed him. "Thank you," he murmured so lowly that Kris could barely hear him, "for giving yourself to science." Then he scooped a scalpel up and dragged the tip across Trevor's wrist. A ribbon of red appeared, rushing down the man's palm then fingertips before finally draining into an awaiting pail.

Kris looked away, but the smell of the blood threatened to make him ill.

"I woke you so you could help me, not so you could stand and gawk at the floor." Waving the bloody scalpel, his father motioned to the brown liquid on the counter. "Take the blood and pour it into that mixture. Don't spill it; it's the life force that will bring the automaton to life."

Kris glanced around the table, found a pair of gloves, and tugged them on. Obediently, he took the pail of blood and replaced it with another pail before he returned to the workspace where the mixture awaited. With a furrowed brow, he poured it into the tall beaker. The blood roiled at the fresh addition, then settled.

"Good," his father said from behind him. "Begin pouring it into the machine."

Kris looked over his shoulder, a question on his lips as to where to pour it, but he could see a funnel with a long tube traveling into the automaton's back. Carrying the mixture over, he poured it into the funnel. The dark liquid zigzagged through the rubber hose until it settled into the awaiting drum inside.

"The key is to infuse live blood with the compound I created. The compound will fuse to the life force in the blood." Magnus paused, clucking his tongue as he noticed Trevor had passed on. He pulled a sheet up over the man, then shifted his attention toward the machine. He flicked his blood-covered fingers at a panel on the front of the automaton, bringing forth a clicking-whir sound from it.

Kris stumbled back and quickly deposited the tall beaker on the table. He didn't want to be next to whatever abomination was about to spring to life. In jerky movements, the machine twisted its head, arms, and legs, as if testing them out. Dread unfurled in Kris's stomach. What had his father done?

"Yes!" his father bellowed, thrusting a triumphant fist into the air. "I've done it."

But just as quickly as the words had left his mouth, the automaton spasmed. Limbs twisted in on themselves, its head cocked back, and a groaning, human sound escaped the machine, which swiftly turned into a ghastly cry.

Smoke billowed from the creature, then it ceased all movements. Black liquid seeped from the automaton's mouth, looking eerily like blood.

Kris had never heard something so terrifying before. Like a man's dying wail, fused with a banshee's howl.

"What have you done?" His father's voice took on the sharpness of accusation. His pale features turned red as he turned on Kris, fingers curling into a fist.

"M-me?" If he hadn't been half distracted by the horrifying display, Kris would have bolted out the door. As his father's fist connected with his cheek, he fell against the table. Tears burned in his eyes against his wishes—not because he was hurt, but because frustration bubbled within.

If Kris's father had his wits about him, he'd know it wasn't his son's fault, but when Kris chanced a look at him, he knew his father's mind was gone. His eyes were wide, lips pinched in fury. He wasn't *there.* Kris had experienced his father's crazed behavior far more times than he cared to admit. And his physical wrath wasn't anything new either; although as he'd grown older, taller, his father hit him less.

Instead of sticking around, he bolted from the basement, ignoring the howls of displeasure from his father and the slurs that escaped him. He ran as fast as he could up the hall and out of the manor. Tension tightened every one of his muscles. Gone was the heartbreak that swiftly ensued after being struck, and in its place was a hardness, a growing cool indifference to everything about his father.

A footman huffed and twirled on his heel. "Sir, would you—"

"No!" Kris didn't bother to stick around. His feet and long legs carried him through the courtyard and onto the drive, and before long he was running down the cobblestone road toward Emilie's house.

Sweat trickled down his brow and stung his cheek. He lifted a hand, swiping at it only to find blood on his fingertips. Frowning, he shoved the images of the dead man on the table and the writhing automaton from his mind.

Blinded temporarily by his sweat, Kris failed to see a gnarled root on the side of the road. He tripped on it, which sent him sailing forward. He caught himself, hands taking the brunt of the force, but it jarred his shoulders.

Sucking in a ragged breath, he squeezed his eyes shut and refused to think of the horror in his basement.

"Kris, oh my lord, are you all right?" A familiar, soft voice carried to him, but he was focusing on ignoring the flashing images in his mind haunting him. "Kristoph!" Emilie's tone grew panicked when he didn't respond.

He opened his eyes as gentle, gloved fingers probed along his jawline. A soft gasp came from her when she tilted his head up and met his eyes. No doubt the mark on his cheek inspired the look of shock on her face. Without a mirror, he couldn't know how unsightly it was or wasn't. "I'm fine." Kris averted his gaze, clenching his jaw as he buried his feelings deep within.

"No, you're not." She knelt in front of him, shaking her head. "Let's get you into the house and cleaned up. You can tell me what happened . . . if you want to."

In the house? Kris blinked. Confusion rumpled his brow and tilted his lips. When he surveyed the area, he saw the Nilssons' pale yellow house with a red roof. On the wraparound porch, he could make out Emilie's parents, who presently stood at the railing, brows lowered and confusion rumpling their expressions as if they were concerned.

The black iron gate whined as a gust of wind caught it and pulled it open, as if it wished for him to step through too.

"I didn't realize . . . " His words trailed off as Emilie's fingers dragged along his cheek to his jawline and into his hair. Kris's eyes fluttered closed, lulled by the tender, soothing touch. A stark contrast from the punch his father had delivered.

If he could stay in that moment he would have, but they were in the middle of the road, and even Emilie's patient parents would hardly enjoy their daughter making a spectacle of herself.

"Come with me," Emilie prompted again.

And that was all the prompting he needed.

Kris stood, dusting himself off. He'd torn a hole in his slacks and blood stained his linen shirt.

Emilie slid her arm through his and pulled him through the iron gate. "There is still some breakfast out if you—"

"I would love that." He leaned into her, dipping his head down to run the tip of his nose along her ear. "Thank you."

# THREE

Indoors, Emilie led Kris to the sitting room and ran to fetch the first aid kit. An amber bottle with a stained orange-brown cap sat on a dark oak table. Instead of wallpaper, the walls were painted ivory with gold trim, and the far side was painted a deep maroon.

Although it was a stark contrast to the cellar of his family home, the smell of the iodine brought back the dying man's face. Kris grimaced at the intrusive image, wanting nothing more than to blot it away.

When had his father become so sordid? And if his father's blood coursed through him, did that mean Kris would inevitably become just as cold as he was?

"Let me see that," Emilie murmured, dabbing some of the orange liquid onto a cloth. She blotted it along his cheekbone, which pulled a hiss of pain from Kris. "I'm sorry."

"Don't be. It isn't your fault." Kris lifted his hand, his fingers lighting on her wrist. He wanted so badly to tell her why he'd run blindly and fell. But could he? It was known his father wasn't of the soundest disposition. Magnus would throw tantrums if his research didn't go accordingly, and that hadn't changed as long as Kris had been alive.

Emilie's mismatched eyes studied him. She licked her full lips, then cast her glance to the floor. "I want more for you, Kristoph. More than your life with your parents. You know that."

"If I could escape—if we could—I'd run and never look back. The only thing keeping me here is you." Kris caught Emilie's wrist, then brought her hand up so he could brush featherlight kisses against her knuckles.

She sucked in a breath but didn't pull her hand away. Kris placed it against his chest so she could feel the steady thrumming of his heart.

"I would . . ."

There was a *but* that hung heavily between them. He longed for Emilie to continue what it was she was on the verge of saying, but the scuffling of feet outside the room brought his attention away from Emilie's cherubic face. He offered a tight smile to Emilie's mother as she rushed up to the couch he sat on.

Emilie had the same full face as her mother, but where her daughter possessed Ironbark's mark of mismatched eyes, she had a matching pair of blue ones. Despite the fact that she was middle-aged, her skin shone with youth and her blond hair held on to its luster. She frowned, eyes searching his face. "You poor thing. Was this done by—"

"Yes." Kris didn't see a point in lying. The Nilssons weren't unaware of who his parents were or what sort they were. They'd seen a fair share of bruises on his face and arms over the years. "I'm all right."

"I'm sure you are, but Kristoph, you can stay here tonight if you wish. We have the spare room open, and it would allow for things to simmer down." Her voice trailed off, a hint of hopelessness in her tone.

With the windows open, the whistle of the steam engine rolling into the center of town was loud. The ten o'clock engine had arrived and would transport citizens out of Agderland and toward the Vitblek Mountains in the distance and beyond.

Beyond, Kris thought, what a wonderful thing that would be as long as Emilie was by his side.

He caught a look of uncertainty in Mrs. Nilsson's gaze. "I appreciate that, but it isn't necessary." Tentatively, Kris reached out and took a hold of her hand, squeezing it. "Truly. My father will be distraught and holed up in his room now. I won't see either of my parents once I venture home."

"At the very least, you must stay for supper."

A small laugh escaped Kris. "I will take you up on that offer." He followed Mrs. Nilsson's movements as she glided along the floor.

"I'll let the cook know." She offered him a small smile, then left Emilie and Kris alone.

"It's hard to believe that we met quite by accident." He shifted on the couch, making room for Emilie to join him. She sat down, arranging her petticoat and skirt. She leaned into the corner of the couch, smiling at him. "If I hadn't been cross with my mother, I'd never have stumbled on you sobbing over a lost ribbon."

Emilie had been a wreck when he stumbled on her when she was only twelve. Although he couldn't understand why she'd been fussing over a ribbon, Kris had empathized with her distress and he'd helped her find it.

Emilie had looked at him as if he were some hero, when all he'd done was pull the pastel green ribbon from a bush. Little did he know it had belonged to her late grandmother, and the ribbon held fond memories of their time shared; it was only a ribbon to him, but it meant so much more to the little girl.

"It wasn't about the ribbon!" Emilie hissed, thwapping his arm playfully. "It was about who gifted the ribbon to me."

"Oh yes, yes . . . " He lifted a hand and pressed a finger to his lips in thought, but as he glanced down, he saw flecks of blood. Blood that wasn't necessarily his. Kris blanched, his head drooping. "I wish we could go back to then."

"I don't," Emilie was quick to say, "because I'd have to

wait that much longer to spend the rest of my days with you."

Warmth spread through Kris at her words. In the past years, both he and Emilie hinted at deeper feelings, but neither one confessed their feelings to one another. But Kris knew he loved Emilie and knew every time he gazed into her eyes she felt the same way, too. It was in the subtle touches, the way her voice went up an octave when they were in one another's company, and how she encouraged him to be more than a product of his upbringing.

They were more. Weren't they?

"I'm . . . I'm more than an escape, aren't I?" he whispered. Vulnerability was an ugly thing in his family, but Kris couldn't stop his lips from moving.

Emilie's eyes widened. She quickly leaned forward and grabbed both of his hands in hers. Pain entered her gaze, but then her brows lifted. "Kristoph, you are everything I could ever hope for."

She was holding back still. He could hear it in her tone and as he searched her eyes, there was something there, too. "Emilie," he whispered, and pulled one of his hands free. He tucked the tendrils of blond behind her ear. "You are my heart and I love you." The confession spilled out, but he couldn't stop. "Without you, I'd cease. A shell would be left behind, with no soul."

Emilie sucked a breath in, then leaned closer to him. A blush entered her cheeks, and she exhaled shakily. "I love you and have loved you ever since you pulled my ribbon free from the rosebush." She squeezed his hand, glanced over her shoulder quickly, and turned back to him. Without hesitating, her lips clashed with his, unpracticed and innocent.

But heaven help him . . . between the sweet perfume that clung to her and the taste of her mouth against his, Kris wished her parents weren't home. He cupped her cheek, tilting Emilie's head for better access. His tongue swiped along hers, pulling a groan from him. If he could grab her by the hips and pull her on top . . .

Kris interrupted his thoughts and withdrew from her. "I want to, but your parents . . . " He eyed the doorway as if they'd walk in at any moment, and they might have.

Emilie's cheeks burned with desire and it reflected in her eyes, which only added to his discomfort.

One day, she'd be his entirely. Until then, he had to wait.

Emilie lifted her hand and the pad of her thumb dragged along his cheekbone. "You are a good man, Kristoph." She tilted her head, following his gaze as he shifted it away. "Your heart is in the right place all the time."

If Kris could absorb Emilie's purity, he would have. But it would have to be enough to bask in her presence. Her gentleness always seemed to soothe the shadows that lurked within his mind. The same demons that threatened to spread, much like a virus, through him. The older he became, the more he felt the taint of them.

He leaned forward, closing the gap between them, and pressed his lips to hers once again. He savored the taste of her honey lips, allowing her light to spread through him. "Of all the things I've stumbled on in my life, you are by far my greatest find."

"Miss Emilie," a tinny voice called from the doorway. A sleek automaton shifted its position. Then, with a tilt of the head, it walked into the room, far more agile than it should've been. It wasn't a model that boasted humanoid aspects outside of the shape of its body. "For the sake of propriety, please remain at least six inches away from Lord Sevrein at all times." Amber eyes stared at Kris and Emilie like two golden lamps. No skin covered the automaton, no hair. It was just metal.

Kris withdrew from Emilie, his eyes following the machine. At once, Trevor's face floated to the forefront of his mind and his stomach lurched.

Despite the conflict rising within, Kris managed a smile when Emilie huffed.

Emilie twisted and cast a narrowed glance at the automaton. "Moddy, did Mother send you?" In reply, the machine remained silent and still. "Moddy."

Kris leaned against the couch, chuckling to himself. "You know your mother did." Not that he could blame her for sending a machine in to disturb them. But he still didn't appreciate the interruption.

Moddy's neck whirred as she glanced from Emilie to

Kris. "That is correct, young Lord. Miss Nilsson knows it isn't proper for—"

"Oh! Very well." Emilie sprung to her feet and twirled to face him. "Now that we have a chaperone, I suppose we should take advantage of the sun and take a walk." She looked at him through her thick blond lashes and smiled shyly. "If you wanted to stay for supper, that is . . ."

"On both accounts, I'd love to." He stood, offering his arm to Emilie despite the repetitive lecture Moddy hummed. "It would be entirely remiss of me to not offer the young lady an arm. And while you're there, Moddy, surely I cannot be a rascal."

Twin lights peered at him, fading for a moment then lighting back up. The automaton seemed to process what he said, for she stepped back and allowed Kris to lead Emilie out of the room. But Moddy's footfalls were less than stealthy. The machine clopped on the wooden floor as heavily as a horse might.

Emilie locked eyes with Kris. She sighed, leaning into him, and although they weren't alone, unable to explore one another, it was enough for him.

For hours, Kris strolled the streets of Skonstad city with Emilie and clunky Moddy. It had been the only home he knew. A beautiful cityscape set beside the Blatt Sea, with spires that stretched toward the sky and plumes of steam that puffed from the factories, as well as roaring engines.

The cobblestone streets boasted a slick sheen from the

humid air. Even amidst mountains, the warm summer sun wasn't enough to chase away the chill that swept through in the night.

Kris didn't want to move away from Skonstad. But if it meant a happy life with Emilie, he'd do anything he could.

# FOUR

A few days after the failure of binding the soul to the automaton, Kris's father was back to speaking to him. Not that Kris had any desire for it.

How could someone kill another and feel nothing? His father blathered on about the technicalities of the science behind it. That he was still missing one thing, and that was enough to send it all off course.

That was all he cared for, and it should have surprised Kris but it didn't.

"Kristoph," his father called down the hall from the solarium.

If he could have turned into the plant he was tending, Kris would have taken the moment to do just that. But his father slid into the solarium, pale-blue eyes bright and his cheeks flushed. If Kris didn't know any better, he'd think his father was drunk, but he was only frenzied with inspiration or discovery.

"I need you to look over these notes with me." His

father waved the papers around then paused in the doorway. His lips pressed into a thin line as he regarded the plants Kris tended to. "You can play with your things later."

*Things*, he thought bitterly. The *things* his father disregarded were highly sought-after plants, and some were even hybrids Kris had created over the years. No, he didn't toil with rivets, cogs, or gears. He preferred botany above all else.

Over the years, Kris had developed a thick skin when dealing with his father. His words plinked against the armor he'd constructed in his presence, tumbling down to the dirty floor. "Let me see them." He lifted a brow, casting his father a dry glance.

"These aren't them," his father snapped. "These are the errors I've found."

It was difficult to withhold a sneer of his own and brush his father off, but Kris did.

With a sigh, he placed the potted orchid onto the table. Aside from turning to face his father, he hadn't actually made any movements toward him. Glancing down, he picked up a bronze watering can and spritzed a few of the unhappy blooms.

An impatient exhale prompted him to set it back down. He smiled as he rolled up his sleeves and walked up to his father. "What do you need help with exactly?"

When Magnus Sevrein grew cross, his brows furrowed, his lips pinched together, and his eyes looked as if they'd freeze over a room. He looked very much like that, and Kris's amusement mounted. It wasn't every day he could rouse a reaction from his father.

"My notes," he bit out, rubbing the wrinkle between his eyebrows. "Something is amiss. And . . . I need another set of eyes. You've helped me for years. Surely you can spot something?"

"Maybe." Kris shrugged. "But I also have no schooling in Thanatology or reanimation." His expertise didn't lie within the realm of the dead or bringing them back to life. Sighing, Kris looked to the skylights above. The trailing ivy snaked along the iron bars crafted specifically for them, and the palm trees stretched toward the sun's bright rays. His solarium looked more akin to a jungle than a room set off to the side of their home.

His father pinched the bridge of his nose, as if gathering his patience thread by thread. "I just need your eyes, Kristoph."

"So you've said." Kris kept his tone light, even though he felt anything but. Snatching up a cloth, he wiped the dirt from his hands then shoved it into his back pocket before following his father out into the hall.

Upstairs, the sound of glass shattering echoed through the halls, accompanied by a shrill scream. His mother likely ran out of her belladonna, or had been rationing it, because their family physician refused to give it to her any longer.

Muffled voices—the servants'—joined the wailing, pleading with her.

"She isn't feeling her best today, your mother."

His father was keen on making excuses for her, but Kris's well had run dry of them. There were no excuses for either of his parents. He also didn't care whether she felt well. When did she ever think to ask him how he felt?

Down the hall, toward the cellar door, Kris caught a whiff of the chemicals his father used. It burned his nose and smelled of rotten eggs. Nothing in him wished to go down the stone stairs. The memory of the dead man was far too fresh in his mind.

He gritted his teeth as he lingered at the top, but his father's impatient sigh drew Kris down the steps. Couldn't his father have snagged the notes from his work desk and handed them over? Did Kris *have* to venture down—

"Would you cease dragging your feet?"

Behind him, Kris rolled his eyes but hurried down after his father. Did he want to quicken his strides? No, but the sooner he glanced at the notes, the sooner he could run back up the stairs. And as he stepped onto the cellar floor, his eyes immediately went to where the man had died. He was long since gone, but Kris could almost see his body again.

His father rummaged on the desk, pulling Kris's attention away from the table. "What is missing?" He thrust the notebook at him, features as tight as his voice was.

Quietly, Kris flipped through the pages. The script was so familiar, as were the notes. He read over what his father had done, where he'd failed, where there was minor success. Everything he'd done had been right, but as Kris continued to read, he realized there was a key component missing in every test.

Schooling his features, Kris shrugged. "I don't know. It's strange. You've done everything, it seems, but I'm not the right person." Except he was. He'd grown up tinkering as much as his father and just because he hadn't studied the same subjects, didn't mean he hadn't a clue.

Blood needed to bind with the chemicals, but the soul needed a will, and the will needed transportation through the bloodstream to keep the soul pumping through the automaton. Magic didn't exist in their world, but religion did, and it didn't take a scholar in religion to garner that information.

It occurred to Kris that he should tell his father this, but the fact that he'd dragged a poor man into the cellar to kill still disgusted him. And the ease with which he'd so carelessly ended the man's life was enough to chase that thought away. His father didn't deserve to know the missing element.

Pressing his lips together, Kris ran his thumb along his brow, smoothing out any suspicious lines that grew. "Do you mind if I take this upstairs to study it a little?" If he could copy the notes and implant his ideas, he could sell it.

Damn his parents and their wretched ways. He'd have his own money and he could run with Emilie.

A beat went by, his father's eyes narrowing as he considered it. "Very well. Don't keep them too long. I'm ahead of the game still, no one has cracked this. Automatons with personalities are one thing, but containing a human soul is another entirely."

He was right. Countless individuals were attempting to replicate what someone had done only once. None could find that key, but none thought with more than their mind.

"I'll have the notes back to you, but it'd likely be a good thing for you to take a break away from them. Frustration is the worst block for creativity." He grinned, but it faded quickly as his father didn't show any sign of amusement. With another shrug, he turned on his heel. "I'll see what I can do for you."

In the course of two days, Kris had copied down the notes and implemented his additions. An automaton needed life within it. Nanobots, infused with blood and essence, would carry the soul through the alchemical blood mixture, lending life and soul to the machine. His father would've been proud if he saw the addition, but he never would, because the notes weren't for him.

A crackling on Kris's desk snagged his attention. A

small screen glowed gray, then a fuzzy picture grew into focus. Soft blond curls clung to Emilie's skin, and even with the sepia-toned screen, he could tell she was paler than usual.

He knew the doctor would be visiting her today. She hadn't felt right . . . too tired, decreased appetite, and heaviness in her chest.

"Kristoph," Emilie spoke his name softly. "The doctor just left." The words hung in the air for a moment, and she nodded. "It's not looking good. My blood tests are all over the place."

That's not what he wanted to hear, but it was the truth they both had to face. He frowned, dragging a hand through his hair. "I'll find someone to treat you." Desperation clawed at his mind, his heart. He squeezed the pen in his fingers, shaking his head. "I'll do whatever I can for you, Emilie, you know that. If I have to scour the world, I will."

"Kristoph," she murmured, lowering her eyes. "You know what this disease does."

Every muscle in his face tensed. He slammed his fist down on his desk, but his eyes remained soft. He could see them in the reflection on the screen. They were so full of fear, hurt, bitterness, anger. Love. "It won't take you from me. I won't let it, Emilie. We belong together. For always."

Emilie touched her fingers against the screen. "For always." She withdrew her hand, sighing. "I'd like to see you today. Do you think you can?"

Even as Emilie spoke, Kris's mind ran through various scenarios. There was no way that his father would help pay for Emilie's treatments, and even if Kris dipped his fingers into his savings, the moment his father learned of it, he'd surely freeze the accounts.

Uncle Hakon was an option. Unlike Kris's father, Hakon was genuinely kind and possessed a warm heart. Growing up, Kris never had much of a relationship with him, mostly because of his father's prejudices. If he could appeal to him . . .

"How can I deny my lovely rose a visit?" Kris leaned in toward the screen, offering her a smile. "I need to visit someone I haven't seen in a very long time." Tilting his head, he stared through strands of blond. "I'll be over for supper. How is that?"

Emilie's smile grew, adding warmth to her cherubic features. "Lovely. I'll let my parents know an extra plate needs to be set."

"Perfect." He leaned his chin into his palm. "Be sure to save a kiss for me too." Kris could make out the color rushing into her cheeks, which made him grin.

"Kris!" she whisper-yelled at him. "I'll see you soon."

The screen on the device cut out, growing crackly again as the picture faded into grayness. With Emilie not staring at him, his features tightened again. Why, of all people, did his Emilie have to endure Ironbark disease?

Worry weighed him down. He leaned against the back of the chair, stared up at the ceiling, and willed whatever power that lay beyond the heavens to listen. *Help. Help her.*

But if life taught Kris one thing, it was to never wait for someone else to make a move. He shifted, glancing down at the paper that he copied, and scooped up his notebook. It would do no good if his father found it. So he swept it into a drawer on his desk, then locked it.

Hope simmered in his chest. Perhaps his uncle would sympathize with him.

# FIVE

Outside of the Sevrein's family home, steam clouded the sky, blocking the sun's midday rays. It was unfortunate, but given the heat the summer sun had been producing, Kris took the reprieve. Amidst the birds twittering in the trees, the low humming of a passing dirigible caught his attention, then the airship came into view, tugging along a banner that read *Thor Industries. Your new employee awaits.* Thor Industries was Agderland's top company as far as automatons—or any steam machine went. Kris's father was hoping to sell them his soul-imbued patent, if that day ever came.

He rounded the corner of the family home and headed toward a detached building set back from the road. It held the family vehicles. Since horses weren't favored transport any longer, most homes had steam-powered cabs. They were cleaner than horses, far easier on expenses, and the upkeep was cheaper, too.

Kris cranked a wheel, which opened the door slowly.

When it was finally open, he walked toward his cab. It looked similar to a horse-drawn hackney, except it boasted two wheels in the back and one up front. Where the horse should've stood was a steering wheel, and behind the driver's bench hid the rumbling steam engine.

Moving toward the machine, Kris used the step to haul himself up on the maroon velvet cushion. As he sat, he turned the key, watching as the needle on a gauge flew toward the opposite end, signifying the steam was already bubbling within the water tank. A few more seconds and he turned the engine on. It started with a thunderous rumble, then produced a cloud of steam.

As soon as Kris shifted the vehicle out of park, it took off at a steady puttering on the street. If the streets were clear, he'd be at his uncle's within the hour.

The odds were in his favor. No steam hackneys or trollies cluttered the roadway, but it still took nearly an hour to travel toward the countryside of Skonstad.

The air smelled cleaner, fresher out in the rural part of the city. It had a crisp quality to it that was lacking in the metropolitan area. Kris could nearly taste the icy mountain water on his tongue and it made him yearn for a life out here, rather than the claustrophobic setting of the inner city.

Homes dotted the road, but they didn't overshadow

one another. They even possessed more than a note's worth of land to boot. This was what he wanted with Emilie and for their future.

The engine's putting didn't echo off any buildings. It was as if the open air swallowed it up. Kris smiled to himself as he followed the winding road. Fluff from dandelions floated on the breeze in front of him, and he lifted his hand from the wheel to catch some. *Wishes*, he thought. *Emilie always said there were thousands of wishes waiting to be made.*

Opening his hand, he blew as hard as he could, wishing for a lifetime with his beloved rose a thousand times over a thousand.

The machine stuttered as it climbed a hill. Heat from the exhaust wafted over Kris's back, only adding to the sweat that already licked at his brow.

He was nearly there.

Beyond the hill, the Sevrein Estate sat sprawling along its lustrous land. Wildflowers bloomed in various colors, and tall oaks loomed close to the impressive structure.

White-washed stone reflected the sun, temporarily blinding Kris as he looked at it for too long. He had forgotten how unique the mansion was. Spires jutted toward the sky as if they were intent on stabbing it. There were more windows than he could count and on the very top floor, which was the third floor in the house, an expansive balcony stretched across one spire.

Kris steered the steam hackney down the gravel road,

which led him into a small courtyard. He cut the engine, then wiped the sweat from his face. Stretching his long legs, he hopped down and walked up to the front door. Just as he was readying to ring the bell, the door swung open.

No automaton stared at him, but doe-brown eyes set in a middle-aged woman's face did. "Dr. Se—no." She paused, seemingly gathering her wits. Graying blond hair was pulled back into a tight, tidy bun. Recognition dawned on her. "Goodness me, is that you, Lord Kristoph?" Turid, the housekeeper, blinked up at him.

"In the flesh," he said with a grin.

"So I see. Come in." She opened the door wide, allowing him passage. "Your uncle is in his study, if that's who you're here to see."

"It is, actually."

Turid nodded. "Your aunt is in the gardens with the baby."

"Baby?" Kris echoed. Confusion tugged his voice up an octave. *When did Hakon and Saxa have a baby?*

"Yes. Didn't you know? A little girl was born in the spring. Her name is Tindra." Turid waved her hand before placing it on her heart. "The sweetest babe and so good too."

Kris's brows furrowed, but he didn't linger to talk about the newest addition to the family. Unfortunately for Hakon, a little girl wouldn't be inheriting this estate. He frowned, walking through the front hall and toward the breezeway that led to the grand staircase. Upstairs to the right, the study was the first room.

The door was wide open and the first sight he saw was the wall of books. His uncle was at his desk near the massive bay window, head bowed as he read whatever lay in front of him.

Kris rapped his finger on the door frame and waited until his uncle looked up. "Hello, Uncle. I hear congratulations are in order."

Hakon's light-blue eyes lit up. "Kristoph!" He stood from his chair and crossed the room, wasting no time embracing Kris. Unused to such affections, Kris stood awkwardly and patted his uncle on the back. "By the light, I haven't seen you in a while. You look like a man . . . a far more handsome one than your father." He winked.

Kris chuckled. It was odd seeing how light-hearted his uncle could be, while his father was the polar opposite.

"Come, sit." Hakon motioned toward a leather couch against the wall nearest to Kris. The deep red-brown leather complemented the dark-green walls of the study. "Would you care for anything to drink?"

Kris lowered himself, then shook his head. "No, I'm afraid I'm not here for a pleasant reason. I'm here to ask for a favor."

Hakon leaned into the corner of the couch but didn't say a word.

With a frown, Kris continued. "The young woman I wish to marry suffers from Ironbark disease. She's received some troubling news." His hands ran along the top of his knees, then dragged down his thighs. "It's not looking good. There are trial medications out there. If I could tap into my savings then she'd be all set, but I know the moment I do—"

"Your father would freeze the account." Hakon's tone was matter-of-fact, but his familiar eyes held more compassion than Kris expected. "Your father is my brother, but I don't understand him. We were raised the same, and our parents never taught us to be callous or cold." He sighed, scratching between his eyebrows. "I think fear of failure and fear of *life* has warped him. That aside, my boy, I will help you with the treatments, with no strings attached. Sorensen's Pharmaceuticals has created a trial drug. It may be worth considering." He leaned forward, patting Kris's knee. "But tell me something. Are you still into flowers? I need some opinions on the gardens. And while you're out there, you can meet Tindra."

Fatherly pride shone within Hakon's features. He was younger than Kris's father by five years and his wife was only a little younger. Try as they would, it seemed impossible for them to conceive a child—until last year, clearly.

"I did not know you were expecting, but congratulations."

A dark shadow passed over Hakon's eyes, but he said nothing. Kris wondered what it was, if it had to do with

Saxa, and what price the child had come at. They were dark musings. But the world wasn't kind to most.

"Thank you." Hakon nodded, then stood from the couch before motioning to Kris. "Let's check out that garden."

For a half hour they milled around the gardens. Thankfully, Kris hadn't seen his aunt or the baby and thought he was free of that interaction until they rounded the backyard and Kris stopped short before colliding into a body.

A baby with chubby red cheeks blinked up at him from beneath a frilly white bonnet. Kris stared down into the nearly clear blue eyes of the infant, which were so much like his own. Wisps of the lightest shade of blond tickled at her wrinkled forehead.

He'd never proclaimed himself one who enjoyed babies or even knew how to act around them. But she was downright angelic looking.

"You can hold her if you'd like." Saxa shifted Tindra in her arms and offered her to Kris. Before he could refuse, the child had passed from her hands to his.

Awkwardly, Kris held her out, his brows furrowing in discomfort. "Hello, Tindra," he murmured softly, pulling her closer to his chest. She was a robust little thing, able to hold her head up and look around shakily.

It made him wonder, if life were kinder could this ever be a possibility for himself and Emilie? The thought pulled a smile from him and without a word, he returned Tindra to her mother's arms.

"I cannot stay, but I'm sure you'll see me around more often." He bowed his head and continued down the path that led to the courtyard up front. Already, his uncle waited at the machine, tapping on it with his knuckle.

"I don't understand why everything has to be a machine these days." He sighed as he righted himself.

Kris shrugged, propping himself against one of the tall wheels on the rear end of the machine. "It's the way of the world, so it would seem. Humankind complains too much, and they are too self-important to perform various tasks. You rarely hear an automaton complain."

"Spoken like your father." Hakon paused, bowing his head. "I mean no offense, only that he shares a similar view. There is nothing wrong with it."

"I never said I agreed with the view. It's just a fact." Kris's lips thinned as he fought to control a mounting temper. He didn't want to be anything like his father.

Hakon closed the distance between them and planted his hand on Kris's shoulder, squeezing it. "Take care. You have my word that I'll do what I can when you need me. I'll look into Sorensen's trials."

"Thank you again, Uncle." Kris offered a small smile, then climbed into his steam hackney, turned the engine on, and prepared to journey to Emilie's. He had good news at least, and finally someone who would help them.

# SIX

On arrival at the Nilssons' home, Kris could already smell the fragrance of almond cake. It was his favorite dessert, and they always made certain he had plenty of it when he stayed for supper.

Halfway to the door, Emilie emerged onto the front porch and held her hand out. "I've been waiting for you." She wore a pale-blue sleeveless dress with ruffles on the shoulders. It clung to her slender frame, which seemed frailer than usual. Kris didn't want to dwell on it, but it was difficult to distract himself from the truth as it glared at him.

He bowed his head as he gently took her hand in his, then placed a tender kiss to her knuckles. "And here I am." Pulling back, he scanned the windows for spying parents, and when he saw nothing, he scooped Emilie into his arms. He squeezed her gently and peppered kisses along her temple. "I'm famished, but after supper we need to talk."

Emilie closed her eyes as Kris continued to kiss every inch of her face, but when his lips connected to hers, she stiffened, then relaxed in his arms. Her soft lips tasted of almond cake and herbal tea.

"Supper is ready," she murmured against his lips and leaned in for another lingering kiss.

Kris shifted his jaw and sighed. "Very well." His broad shoulders slumped as he took one slow step after the other.

Emilie laughed, tugging on his hand. "Come on." She squeezed her fingers against his. "I've saved kisses for after dessert." Glancing up at him through her lashes, she offered a teasing smile.

It was enough to twist his gut with desire. Kris longed to take her into his arms and claim every part of her as his own. To have her take his name, his body, as much as she took his heart.

"Damn good manners to the depths," he proclaimed as he followed her into the house for supper.

By the time they'd finished eating, the sun had dipped below the mountains and the moon ascended to its throne amidst the velvet night sky. Stars twinkled like diamonds in light, mesmerizing Kris. Beside him on a blanket, Emilie leaned against him, staring up at the sky.

He dragged his knuckles down her cheek, then spread his fingers through her pale blond hair. The strands were like threads of moonlight against his skin—like gossamer. Just as his orchids were delicate, so was Emilie. And yet she was resilient despite what life threw at her.

"I spoke with my uncle." Kris broke the silence. "He agreed to help find treatment. Sorensen Pharmaceuticals has a trial drug . . ."

Emilie withdrew, twisting to face him. Instead of the elation he figured she might display, her brows furrowed in confusion. Almost as if she were displeased. "Kristoph, I don't know."

"Don't know what? It could alleviate all of your symptoms from Ironbark, it could even—" Emilie's fingers against his lips silenced him and a knot of emotion formed in his chest, throbbing. Did she not want to be well? Did she not want to be with him?

"All I've ever wanted is a life with you. But you deserve more, Kristoph. You deserve to not worry if I catch a cold, if it'll be my end. Or if I don't eat a proper meal, if it'll send my body into rebellion. I want that for you because I love you."

He didn't like the tone of her voice, as if she'd all but given up and resigned herself to a shortened lifespan. Frowning, he turned to her and cupped her face. "Emilie, you are my very breath. There will only ever be one you, do you hear me? One you and one love."

She grabbed his wrists, squeezing. "No. There will be more life for you. Understand this: I don't want you to cease living when I draw my last breath. You will continue to live and learn to love again."

Kris didn't understand. Was this her goodbye? "Emilie?"

"I will fight as long as I can, and so I'll try the trial drug, but know this . . . When my time comes . . . let me go." Her voice broke as she spoke the words. Leaning forward, she pressed her forehead against his.

Panic gripped at Kris, and he pulled backward. "Marry me. Not tomorrow, but soon. Marry me."

"Kris, my father . . . " she whispered, withdrawing from him. "You know what he's said, and you know he wants us to wait for my birthday."

He frowned, knowing fully well what her father thought. But maybe with the news he'd be more forgiving. Kris hoped, anyway.

"I'll ask then. I won't know unless I ask . . . again." His lips twisted into a sardonic smile. Could life simply let him have one thing? Just one. He'd give away his wealth and the clothes off his back in trade for Emilie's health.

Emilie sighed, relaxing or simply letting the topic go. She settled into his side once again and before long, she drifted off into a light slumber. Her head rested against his chest as they lay on the blanket. But while she slept, Kris wished on a thousand stars.

A splatter of rain against his cheek disturbed his wishes. There were few clouds in the sky; it was likely a passing cloud. Not wanting to rouse Emilie, he scooped her up into his arms and carried her into the house. She was in a deeper sleep than he thought, for she didn't wake when he ascended the stairwell and brought her into her room.

When Kris came downstairs, Mr. Nilsson nodded. "I think we need to talk." He motioned toward the sitting room, pipe in his other hand.

"Yes, sir, we do." Kris followed him toward the room and sat in a chair. "She was tired."

"And will continue to grow more tired as the days pass." He frowned, opting to stand near the bay window. Rain pelted against it, sending rivulets coursing down the glass. "Her results weren't good today. I know you love her nearly as much as I do, and she feels strongly about you as well—"

"Pardon, Mr. Nilsson, but I'm keen on speaking straightforwardly." Kris ran his hands along his thighs, gripping his knees tightly. Would any of the wishes he made come true? There was one he could test. "I'd like to ask Emilie to be my wife. I know you've said on her eighteenth birthday, but with just under six months to go and with tomorrow not being promised . . ." He clasped his hands together, bowing his head as his throat bobbed with emotion. "With all due respect, I'd like to marry your daughter with or without your blessing."

Mr. Nilsson's lips twitched, his expression unreadable for a moment, and then he laughed. It sounded tired— hollow. "With or without my blessing," he echoed.

"Kristoph, you're as much a son to me as Emilie is my daughter. I give you my blessings because I know that every day is a gift."

Kris nodded. "My uncle has agreed to help pay for some treatments. Sorensen has trials for a new drug that allegedly weakens the effects of Ironbark. I told Emilie about it, and she wishes to try it." He omitted the fact that she'd sounded defeated outside, as if the end was already near.

Mr. Nilsson moved away from the window and took a seat in a chair across from Kris. "A trial . . ." His eyes darted toward the ceiling as he sighed. "Thank you." His tone was tight, as if he were trying not to cry. Clearing his throat, he rubbed beneath his eye and tossed his pipe into the dish on the end table near him. "It's raining. Please stay the night in the spare room."

Kris wanted to speak more on it, but Mr. Nilsson's weary expression and the distant look in his eyes told him it was his cue to leave. Even Kris felt exhausted enough to retire to bed early.

Weeks, not days, passed by before Sorensen Pharmaceuticals finally reached out to Emilie about the trials. With only four more months until her birthday, Kris had a lot to think about. He'd nearly paced straight through his bedroom's flooring as he dwelled on what to do. In the end, he commissioned a gold ring with diamonds crafted into a flower.

But with each passing week, it never felt as though it were the right time. Not wanting to waste a minute more, he pocketed the ring box on the day he accompanied Emilie to her appointment.

She stood by his side, wearing a cream-yellow dress with a brown leather belt cinching it. It clung to her frail figure and lent her a ghostly glow. "Do you think this will work?" Emilie's voice came softly. Uncertainty and hopefulness laced her tone.

Kris wanted to say without a doubt it would, but he was ever a pragmatic man. "There is only one way to find out, and if not, think of all the time you get to spend with me." He winked as he slid his hand down her back and to her hip.

She turned to face the building in front of them. It looked more like a church than a pharmaceutical company. Windows lined the first level, spanning from floor to ceiling, and a single spire jutted toward the sky. As long as Kris had been alive, it'd always been Sorensen Pharmaceuticals, but perhaps before then it'd been a place of worship.

"Shall we, my rose?" Kris smiled down at Emilie, and when she nodded, he escorted her into the building.

The inside had vaulted ceilings that didn't argue with the notion that the building was, in fact, a church in a previous life. And the windows that spanned across the walls lent it so much natural lighting, it bleached out the rooms and gave it a sterile feeling. Like a hospital.

"Good afternoon," a woman at the front desk greeted, far too chirpy. Her smile was as white as the uniform dress she wore. "Who is checking in?" She blinked owlishly and glanced between him and Emilie.

"I am." Emilie moved forward and looked down at the sign-in sheet. "Emilie Nilsson," she stated as she wrote her name down.

"Very well. Thank you, Emilie. You may have a seat, and someone will call you." The woman turned her attention to the typewriter in front of her and continued working.

Emilie didn't say a word. She never did when she was nervous. Instead, she picked at her short nails and ran the toe of her boot along the heel of her other foot.

Kris laid his hand on top of hers and squeezed. "I am here. No matter what." He lifted their hands and kissed her fingertips.

She blushed at the show of affection in public, but Kris didn't give one lick about what anyone else thought.

"I just don't want to get my hopes up." She paused, then added, "*Our* hopes."

"Emilie Nilsson," a man's voice called from the hallway. His dark curls were plastered against his head, and it took a moment for Kris to figure out what was so unsettling about him, but then he homed in on it. One eye was a light shade of green, while the other was surrounded with bronze. In the very center, a dark-green iris whirred as it focused on them.

Kris watched in fascination as the mechanical iris expanded then closed of its own accord, adjusting with the lighting of the room. No doubt it was one of Thor Industries' pieces.

Emilie was the first to stand, then Kris followed as she approached the man. "That is me," she offered softly.

The man smiled. "Ah, so good to meet you." He extended his hand in greeting, bowing his head. "I am Dr. Sorensen, the head of the trials, amongst other things."

"Other things, such as running a pharmaceutical company?" Kris's tone was flat. There was something about the man he didn't like and although he couldn't put his finger on it, the gut feeling was there. He lifted a brow and grudgingly shook his hand after Emilie.

"Kristoph Sevrein." Even as he said the name, he could see Sorensen's eyes widen a fraction.

"Magnus's boy," Sorensen stated then turned on his heel, opting not to say any more, which only irritated Kris.

If Sorensen knew his father on a first name basis, it meant they'd shared the same circle at one point. Of course, Kris's father had never spoken about Sorensen outside of whatever was in the paper.

But considering Sorensen was highly successful and Kris's father was still tinkering in their cellar, he could gather why his father never spoke of the doctor.

It was Emilie's turn to squeeze his hand, to calm him.

Dr. Sorensen led them into a room. It didn't look like a typical office room. They had furnished it with an oversized couch with plush green cushions. A stained glass floor lamp stood next to it. Several rows of ceiling-high bookshelves lined the wall and next to a window sat a leather medical chair.

The doctor motioned toward the couch, and he walked to the desk near the door. "Have a seat." The spot between his brows wrinkled as he glanced down at the file on his desk. "I've had a chance to go over your medical files, Emilie, and . . . your results are alarming."

# SEVEN

Kris's heart thundered in his ears. He slid his fingers through Emilie's and squeezed her hand to stop her from picking at her nails. Her rose-colored lips were a sickly pale and the skin beneath her eyes was bruised with shadows.

Had her results differed so greatly from just a few weeks ago?

"I compared yesterday's results to when you first reached out to us, and it's astonishing how rapidly your case is progressing." Dr. Sorensen shook his head and drummed his fingers on his desk. He looked at Emilie like one would a formula or a thesis. She was neither, and Kris wanted to charge him, slam him against the wall, and throttle him.

Was his anger misdirected? Surely, but acting on it might have made him feel better.

Emilie worried at her bottom lip. "What does that mean?"

"It means we need to act quickly. We use the NV1

drug to essentially lull the disease into a deep slumber. Right now, it isn't a fix, just enough to buy us some time to figure out how the drug affects the disease. If we can learn to suppress it . . . we have a hope of creating a new treatment that will effectively put the disease into remission."

Emilie nodded. Although she smiled, Kris could tell it was out of anxiety, not out of politeness or even hope. He couldn't imagine how she felt because he could scarcely grasp the strands of his emotions.

"The first few treatments are administered intravenously, and we would prefer Miss Nilsson stay over for observation."

"I'd like to continue forward," she confirmed, to which Dr. Sorensen replied by offering her a folder of paperwork.

"I'll need you to look over this and sign on the dotted lines."

Emilie glanced over at Kris as if to ask, *Where do we begin?* Kris wished he had the words, but they didn't come. He only hoped that his eyes conveyed, *Here, right here.*

Shakily, she took up a pen, reading along with Kris. Nothing stood out to him as absurd. It was all fairly simple literature stating the company wasn't at fault, this was a trial, and they made no promises as to remission or recovery.

After they read through, Emilie signed the paperwork.

Kris turned his gaze to the doctor. "May we have luncheon before Emilie is admitted?"

"Absolutely. Once you're done, just check in at the desk and we'll be ready for you, Miss Nilsson." Dr. Sorensen pushed away from his desk and extended his hand to Kris. "We are hopeful that this will work."

*Hopeful.* Kris gritted his teeth and turned for the door, escorting Emilie out. She cast her eyes downward, remaining far too quiet as they walked down the long hallway.

"What is it?" Kris prompted.

"I'm thankful. It's just . . . what if it's for nothing?" Emilie's voice sounded hollow. "What if . . . I'm taken away from you, anyway?"

To that, Kris had so many words jumbling in his head, but only a few came out. "I'd fight tooth and nail to bring you back."

Emotions swirled within her gaze. Fear, hope, love. But she grew quiet once again and remained so as they walked through the streets of Skonstad.

A dirigible hummed above them, and the faint sound of a loudspeaker from the airship crackled. Another tour for visitors who were passing through or purposely staying in the technological capital of the world.

All of the technology and still no way to stop Ironbark from advancing. Kris's lips tensed into a sneer.

"Oh, look," Emilie began. "They have meatballs at this stand." She tugged him along to the stall, the smell of spices and sauce wafting toward him. The sun beat down on them; it was too hot to eat steaming meatballs, but Emilie wanted them. "Extra lingonberries, please." Her eyes lit up with excitement. The first flash of life he'd seen all day, and it made Kris chuckle that it was for food, of all things.

Across from the food stand, the city park bustled with life. Children flew kites, couples played Kubb on the lawn. Kris picked at his food, not hungry but suddenly anxious. The ring box in his pocket might have been a lead weight for as heavy as it felt.

Leading Emilie to a bench where they could eat, he sat down and set aside his food. For someone usually so composed and unwilling to show his nerves, he was doing a poor job of concealing them. Even Kris knew he was fidgeting.

"Emilie—"

"Kris, are you all right?" She turned to face him, features pinched as suspicion or worry grew.

"I'm all right, I assure you." He slid from the bench, kneeling on the ground. Slowly, he extracted the box from his pocket. "Emilie, I love you no matter what. In sickness, health, better and worse. I will be your champion and fight with and for you." He revealed the ring nestled inside, the diamonds catching the sun's rays enough to make them glitter. "Will you marry me?"

Emilie gasped, clutching her chest. Shock filtered into

her gaze, happiness, then she frowned and slid her fingers beneath his chin. "But my father . . ."

Kris's heart roared in his ears at the frown, but his worries faded at her words. "Already handled that. We have his blessing."

Tears shimmered in Emilie's eyes. "Truly?" She dropped her hand, offering it to him instead.

"I have never been so certain of something in my life."

"And I've never been so certain when I say yes." She wiggled her fingers at him, smiling as he slid the ring on. "But promise me this . . ."

"Emilie," he hissed, but her eyes implored him to listen.

"Don't dwell on the bad." Emilie leaned forward and pressed a soft kiss to his lips.

Was that truly what she was going to say? Kris didn't believe it. But he allowed himself to bask in the moment and soak up the goodness that radiated from Emilie.

Every good thing must come to an end, and in Kris's life, goodness never lasted. Emilie's treatments began, and the drug made her ill almost immediately, but her numbers remained steady as far as her lab work went.

The first week, she remained in the Institute. The second week she spent regaining her strength, and the third week she was finally herself again. The color returned to her cheeks, the bruising beneath her eyes lessened, and she longed to use the strength she regained to dance with Kris as she used to.

Kris spent as much time as he possibly could with Emilie, and when he was forced to return home, he did his best to avoid his father.

Unfortunately, he couldn't avoid his father on a particularly wretched afternoon. A gnawing anxiousness had hatched within Kris, growing with each passing day. His father always seemed to amplify this, so when he sat at the breakfast table with a smug look on his face, Kris knew a storm brewed.

"You're wasting your time and efforts with that girl." It was the same tiresome insult repeatedly. When Kris said nothing and only crammed a piece of bacon in his mouth, his father continued, "She'll be dead next month."

That was it. Kris slammed his fists on the table, bolting from his seat to loom over his plate. "Shut your mouth, you old coot. You know nothing of Emilie's health."

Magnus scooped his spoon up nonchalantly and dug into his fruit bowl. "On the contrary, I know everything about her health." His eyes narrowed as he looked at his son. "Did you know that before I married your mother, Vidar Sorensen had been vying for her hand?" He shook his head, sighing. "He was the top of the class in our university days, and I was second to him, but I won your mother in the end."

What relevance did this have? Kris rolled his eyes as

his father took a stroll down memory lane, which only served to frustrate him further. "I don't care about your glory days."

"You should because, you see, Vidar told me that you're paying for Emilie's treatments, which isn't true because you haven't touched your accounts. So that means you're getting money from somewhere else, and a little birdy told me that my traitorous brother is doing that. How clever of you, Kristoph."

Kris shoved the chair out of his way, readying to leave the room and not play his father's sordid game, but then his father spoke again.

"Emilie will be dead by the end of summer. I don't know what lies Vidar is feeding you, but her numbers are plummeting rapidly. He needs the funds to continue the trials, but her chemistry has rejected the drug." The smug look remained on his face, his unrepentant words like a dagger to the heart.

"You lie." Kris's voice came in a harsh whisper.

His father sat there, so composed, so calm . . .

"No. I spoke to him yesterday about treatment for your mother, and imagine my surprise when he mentioned seeing my son." He waved his hand toward Kris.

Rage boiled over and before Kris knew it, he stood in front of his father, fists clenching the front of his shirt. "Then why didn't he tell us? You're lying!"

His father's brows dipped downward, and his face

turned a deep crimson. "I am not! Her kidneys are shutting down—already, her heart is weakening."

A low keening emitted from Kris as he slammed his father back against the chair. He didn't want to believe him. He wanted it to be a wicked lie, but there was no tell showing at his father's jaw or eye.

Relinquishing his hold on him, Kris withdrew and turned his back to his father. "If what you say is true, Sorensen will never forget my name." He quickly exited the dining room, rubbing at his eyes as tears burned them.

Kris moved his hand to his chest. It ached as if someone were twisting his heart. He realized he was sucking in breath rapidly, and he sank to his knees. He splayed his hands on the black-and-white tile, gasping for breath that wouldn't come.

Emilie couldn't die. She was his love, his light. Everything that was good in him.

He lifted a hand to swipe at a trail of tears, then swallowed them back and stood to his feet. There would be time for tears, but for now . . . Sorensen needed to be dealt with.

# Eight

Upon arrival at the pharmaceutical company, Kris stormed inside, ignoring the woman at the desk, and charged straight for Sorensen's office. He was nearly there when Mr. Nilsson approached him, his eyes bloodshot, as if he'd been crying.

"Kristoph?" he asked softly. "We tried reaching you. It's Emilie . . . she collapsed at home and we rushed her here."

"Emilie," Kris rasped. "Where?" He followed him down the hall and rushed into the room. Emilie was already hooked up to several lines, one of which pumped fluids into her. She was awake, looking out the window, but her cheeks were hollow and the light in her gaze seemed clouded. He eased toward the bed and grasped her hand. "My rose . . ."

Kris had been so focused on hope that he hadn't noticed how her skin had returned to its gray pallor, or that the bruising beneath her eyes had returned. She was declining and if he hadn't been so foolish or ignorant, perhaps another course could've been taken.

Emilie lifted her other hand, placing it on his. The ring on her finger gleamed in the bright light of the room, seemingly mocking Kris. "You came."

"Of course I did. I'll always come for you." He leaned down, pressing a kiss to her brow. It was cool to the touch. Frowning, Kris peered over his shoulder as metal met the tile flooring.

A whir, then a click as a nurse automaton entered the room. "It is time for your vital check," came the tinny voice. With another series of clicks and whirring, the androgynous figure rounded the hospital bed.

"Isn't the doctor coming in?" Kris asked tightly.

"No." The nurse didn't look at him and its cool tone raked along his nerves, only adding fuel to the fire burning below the surface.

"No?" he asked incredulously and stiffened. "I'll be back, Emilie, get some rest." He bent to kiss her again, glaring at the automaton, then bolted out of the room, not bothering to look at the weeping Mrs. Nilsson.

No doubt they knew the truth or something close to it. The one time Kris wished his father spouted lies was now.

Charging down the hallway, he swung Sorensen's office door open with such force it slammed into the wall, puncturing it with the doorknob. He was ready and caught it as it kicked back toward him. Sorensen leaped up from his seat, recognition dawning on his face. He was tense, his fingers curling toward his palms as he stood, much like a caged animal.

Kris's tall and lean figure dwarfed Sorensen. There was nowhere for him to go, except for calling for security, but as Kris launched over the desk, he curled his fingers around the doctor's white coat and slammed him against the wooden surface.

"You insolent fool," Kris snarled as he yanked the man up, only to smash him down against the desk again. "You knew . . . you knew all along." He could scarcely hear the bellowing coming from Sorensen as he continued to smash him against the desk. Finally, Kris shoved him with enough force that he fell against the wall.

Blood streamed down Sorensen's face and into his mouth. "I did, but it's for the greater good."

"The greater good," Kris echoed, curling his fingers into his palm. He shook with all the rage that had built within him. "I'm tired of hearing what is or isn't for the greater good. You've filled my head with lies and given not only me but Emilie false hope as well. All for what . . . money?"

Sorensen held a hand out. "Stop. It isn't just for money. That money is fueling research for NV1 to improve the success rate."

"No more lies, Sorensen. My father told me you're taking more than just our money. Selling lies and hope to anyone desperate enough to believe it." Kris paced back and forth, jamming his fingers into his hair. "I will ruin you. I will bring your company down . . . " His eyes dropped to the floor, where a cracked picture frame looked up at him. Kris bent over and picked it up. In the sepia-toned picture, he saw Sorensen and a curly-headed boy around the age of seven. "You will be a curse to your son. Shame will follow him and you like a shadow."

He threw the picture frame against the wall then turned his back to the doctor. "Is it true she won't last through the summer?" Kris didn't hear any shuffling, but he cursed as something smashed against the side of his head.

A hot stream flowed over his eyes and when he touched it, blood came away on his fingers. He pivoted on his heel and grabbed Sorensen by the throat, squeezing hard. It would have been so easy to snuff the life out of him.

Sorensen squeaked, gagged, and attempted to claw at Kris's face.

"I didn't hear you, Sorensen. Is it true?" Kris squeezed harder, then tossed him to the floor. Now that his vocal cords were inflamed, he wouldn't be able to talk. *Damn it all.* He glanced down at Sorensen and caught him nodding quickly.

"Dr. Sorensen," a robotic voice called. "Patient Nilsson—" The automaton glanced around the room, assessing the situation before zeroing in on Kris. "I'll page security."

"Don't." Kris took a threatening step forward. "What about Nilsson?"

"She is in heart failure. Kidney function is critically low and her heart—" The automaton couldn't finish because Kris shoved it out of the room and into the hallway wall.

He ran back to Emilie's room and rushed to her bedside. Although his anger didn't subside, it moved out of the way as grief blossomed and lodged a sob in his throat. "Why you?" Kris sat on the bed next to her, lowering his head against her shoulder. "Why not me? I cannot live without you."

Emilie's arm wrapped around his back, and she lifted a hand to cup his cheek. "Yes you can, and you will. You've been the best part of my life for as long as I've known you." She touched the blood on his face, frowning. "I need you to live for me, for the both of us. Do you understand?" She used the sleeve of her gown to wipe away the droplets of blood. "Don't fall back on anger. You're better than that. I love you."

But he wasn't. Kris knew that. Anger gnawed at him like a beast trying to escape its cage.

"It isn't fair." He cupped her hand in both of his and kissed her knuckles. "We belong together." Her eyes fluttered shut and her body relaxed into the mound of pillows behind her as she dozed.

A thought scraped at Kris's mind. If the life he had

mapped out with Emilie didn't come to pass, then he would craft a semblance of one himself.

In a matter of days, Emilie's health declined so steadily that he was certain this was the end. However, as evenly tempered as Emilie was, she was stubborn through and through and the way her body clung to life was a sign of that. She wanted to live—she had the will to live.

As the nurse automaton clanked into the room, it assessed Emilie's vitals. "Patient Nilsson won't be waking. We offer our condolences." It paused for a moment, its amber eyes blinking rapidly. "I've contacted her parents." With that, the cool creature left the room.

This was it . . . Kris crawled into the bed next to Emilie, his arms embracing her tightly as he buried his face in her neck. "Please don't leave me. I cannot bear it. I love you . . ." His voice cracked as he dissolved into a fit of sobs.

How long he laid there with his arms around Emilie, he didn't know. He'd been able to say goodbye, but as her fighting body still lay there, unwilling to pass, a thought niggled at him again.

Kris glanced around the room. The Nilssons would return soon, but for now the room was empty, leaving him alone. In the corner of the room sat a phlebotomist's cart. Small vacuum-sealed containers lined the top of the tray, and sterile needles were wrapped in cloth.

"I will have you, one way or another, my rose. Perhaps not as I intended . . ." Rigidly, Kris scooped up a tube, a needle, and a strap. With one more glance to the door, he turned to Emilie. "We will be together again." He set the vacuum container in place, adjusting the needle before he drew Emilie's blood. Once he was through, he pressed a soft kiss to her cool lips and tasted her for the last time.

Kris pocketed the container and left the room.

He hadn't been home in days. Listening to his father laugh or proclaim that he was right hadn't been on the top of Kris's list. There was no part of him that wanted to deal with his father's callous behavior or his mother's moods if she was awake long enough.

But now he needed his father's cellar and the tools within.

Charging into his room, he pulled out the hidden notebook. Immediately, a shadow formed on his bedroom floor, and a knot grew in his stomach.

"The prodigal son returns." His father scoffed. "What did you do to Sorensen? He canceled your mother's treatment." It sounded more like an inconvenience to him than anything. Not that Magnus actually worried for his wife, or about what would happen if she continued to abuse her medication.

"What he had coming to him." Kris shoved past his father but growled as he was yanked back. They stood eye to eye, glowering at one another. "I don't care what happens to that woman. She has never once been a mother to me. You're barely a father to me, so let's hope what I'm about to do works, and then for once in your life, you'd have done something for me."

Magnus's eyes widened. "What?" Glancing down at the notebook in Kris's grasp, he sneered. "Did you steal my notebook?"

"No, I made notes of my own." Kris stripped his sports jacket off and tossed it across his bedroom, then stormed out into the hall. He gripped the notebook under his armpit and rolled up the sleeves to his shirt. The sound of his shoes slapping against the tile resonated in the quiet house.

"You did what?"

# NINE

"You wanted me to glance over your notes, so I did. And I found some inconsistencies and had theories of my own. I suppose we'll see if it works." Kris ignored his father the rest of the way into the cellar. Of course the lamps were lit; he'd likely been in his hole when Kris had arrived.

But Kris wasn't here to set his father in his pram and entertain him. He set to searching for the nanobots his father stored away. The ones he found resembled pollywogs. Tails stuck out from behind the rounded bodies, which would propel them through the fluid running through the automaton. But the tiny bots needed a life force infused with them, too.

Pulling out the cylinder of blood, Kris carefully injected the entire container of bots with the fluid. Once completed, he turned to the automaton, which hung limply from the ceiling. His father had repaired it over the weeks.

"If this works, it belongs to me." Kris narrowed his eyes on his father, who nodded emphatically. "Where is the alchemical fluid?"

His father grabbed the oversized beaker of fluid and dropped it in front of Kris, who scooped up the nanobots then plunged them into the liquid.

Kris waited a moment then retrieved the remote that controlled the bots. His heart thundered wildly. Every nerve was on end, because if this worked . . .

He carried the beaker toward the automaton and poured the contents into the tube connected to it. The muddy liquid zig-zagged through the line until it collected inside the automaton's belly.

"Breathe," he said to himself, then pushed the button on the remote. Perhaps the universe smiled at him that day, or maybe it was the thousands of wishes made on dandelions and stars. Kris would say it was fate rewarding him.

As he pressed the button, the automaton whirred to life. Not with jerky movements, but with as much grace as the model could muster. Its eyes, unlike the amber glow they had been before, were a soft blue. Kris hadn't replaced the bulbs and surely his father hadn't either.

A string of curses emitted from his father. "You did it!"

"Wh-what is my name?" the automaton craned its head to look at Kris then at his father, its metallic mouth slanting into a smile. Its voice was female, but it didn't sound like the one he yearned to hear, which was likely for the best.

"Your name . . . " Kris choked out, "is Rose." *His sweet rose.* And yet not. This machine wasn't Emilie, and he knew that, but he'd successfully fused the automaton with a human. What that meant, he didn't know.

"Rose. I like that. But am I prickly?" it asked, so curious, so sweet. So like Emilie.

Kris couldn't help himself. He reached out to touch the automaton's cheek. It looked him in the eyes as if some part of it—her—recognized him. "No. I am the prickly one, thorns and all."

After the exchange, he unplugged Rose from the wires, allowing her body to clunk to the floor. She landed on her feet, unsteady at first, then she found her center.

This was different from the horror Kris had witnessed with the automaton before. This one had been imbued with a part of Emilie.

"I cannot believe you did that," his father said from behind him. "How?"

Kris shifted his jaw. He leveled a glare at his father. "You'll never know, because you will not be the one claiming my work." As soon as the crisp words left his lips, his father's face grew red once more. Perhaps his father longed to shake him senseless, but even he knew better than to push Kris right now.

"Don't be so cross with me, boy. It was your uncle who

referred you to Sorensen, after all. He isn't as pristine as you think."

Some people were born skilled weavers, others poets, but Kris's father was born with a barbed tongue that he knew how to wield. He used it to plant noxious seeds within a person. Even if Kris thought nothing of his desperate attempt to rile him and turn him against another in that moment, it would later prove successful on Magnus's part.

"Rose," Kris called softly. "Come with me." He collected the cylinder, notebook, and anything his father may want to peer into, then left the cellar. Behind him, the soft clicking whirrs of the automaton moving followed him.

At the top of the stairs, the head housekeeper frowned at him. "You had a phone call a moment ago . . . It's Emilie, she . . . Oh, I'm so sorry, Master Kristoph . . . She's gone." Ebba dabbed her eyes with a tissue. "Such a beautiful soul she was."

If Kris had known she'd pass so soon, he'd never have left her. A knot lodged itself in his throat, and he closed his eyes. A hand lighted on his shoulder, but it held no warmth. Instead, it was cool.

"Prickly one, are you all right? I sense . . . a sizable amount of sadness in you." Rose shifted, tilting her head to better look at Kris's profile.

Perhaps it was his imagination, but he almost heard an inflection of emotion within her voice. "No. I'm not." Kris waited to see if Rose would act, but silence stretched between them. "I've lost someone very special."

"Do you require assistance finding them?" It was an innocent question, and it held so much damnable hope. As if Rose could bring back Emilie as simple as that. Tears burned his eyes at the thought.

Turning to face Rose, he gazed into the illuminated blue eyes. They weren't Emilie's for they weren't mismatched, or even human-like, but they shone with more concern than his father had ever shown him.

"You won't be able to find her, Rose. Not where she went." Kris pinched the bridge of his nose, squeezing his eyes shut as fresh tears streamed down his cheeks.

"Oh. I am here if you need my help." She stepped beside him, her metal frame still shorter than him.

What came next was something Kris wished he didn't have to do: he needed to see Emilie and the Nilssons. With a funeral now on the horizon, there was much to be planned, and Kris wanted none of it.

But he was there for the Nilssons, who had shown him far more love than his parents ever had, and he was there for Emilie's funeral. Where they played her favorite high-spirited song on a harpsichord and threw rose petals onto her coffin.

Kris had been present for it all, and the one moment he wished he wasn't was when Mr. Nilsson placed the rose diamond ring in his palm.

"She loved you so," was all he said.

And what more could Kris say to that? Because he knew with all his heart how much she loved him, how much he loved her.

Still, it wasn't enough.

# EPILOGUE

In the weeks after Emilie's passing, Kris turned his attention away from the solarium, proclaiming to Rose it was a bitter reminder of what no longer was. She didn't understand, but when he'd explained it, she yearned to know more of a human's complex emotions.

It hadn't been exactly what he wanted to hear, but he indulged the curious automaton and divulged as much as he could, answering questions as she spat them out.

Despite how much Kris detested his father's obsession with mechanical things, it was what occupied most of his days. He'd gone out and purchased the latest artificial flesh for Rose, opting to use a sun-kissed complexion. Then came the dark-blond wig that he strategically glued onto her scalp. By the time Kris was finished, Rose looked as human as possible. But her eyes still weren't quite right.

For a week straight, he tinkered in his room until he fashioned the robotic eyes to perfection. When he placed them into her sockets, she blinked slowly, lowering the lashes he'd attached.

"Do I look pretty?" Rose asked, using her smooth voice that Kris had worked on too.

For the first time in weeks, he smiled. She was beautiful. "Very much so." She smiled at him, which twisted his heart. Rose looked so much like Emilie, and yet not. Emilie without the weight of Ironbark, without the exhaustion and not knowing if she'd live to see another day.

"Now what?" Rose ran one of her fingers along the frill of her dress's sleeve.

The smile Kris wore vanished. "Now, we uphold my promise and ensure Sorensen falls. And we'll pay a brief visit to my uncle too."

# ACKNOWLEDGMENTS

Thank you for reading Kris and Emilie's story! Originally, this wasn't meant to come out until many moons from now, because it's actually a prequel to an upcoming novel I had planned. But, the idea for an anthology came about and I knew just the story I wanted to write, and it was this one.

A huge thanks to Candace, Jacque and Christis for beta-reading this for me! Gossamer & Thorns owes a lot to you.

Big thank you to Brenna of BookMarten Editorial for editing this story for me as well. You always make my stories shine in the best way possible.

Thank you Christis Christie, for loving Kris way before this story was ever written. You're his biggest fan.

Last, but not least, to my patreon supporters, Donna and Sanem, thank you so much! You don't know how much I appreciate your support and cheerleading.

# THE OFFICIAL PLAYLIST

*Want to listen along while you read and immerse yourself into the world of Gossamer & Thorns? Listen to the playlist below!*

1. Sleepsong by Bastille
2. Devilside by Foxes
3. Broken Glass by Sia
4. Dreamweaver by J2
5. The Dark of You by Breaking Benjamin
6. Unchangeable Love by Juniper Vale
7. In Your Arms by Ryan Louder
8. Become the Beast by Karliene
9. Found by Trenton
10. If Not With You, For You by Kris Clifford

Elle Beaumont loves creating vivid and fantastical worlds. She lives in southeastern, Massachusetts with her husband and two children. When not writing or chasing around her children, she enjoys making candles. More than once she has proclaimed that coffee is the lifeblood and it is how she refrains from becoming a zombie.

*Stay up to date and receive some free books by signing up for her newsletter!* ellebeaumontbooks.com/newsletter

*Join Elle's Facebook group and hang out with her* facebook.com/groups/ElleBeaumontStreetTeam

**For more information visit**
**www.ellebeaumontbooks.com**
**Follow Elle on social media!**

 facebook.com/ellebeaumontbooks

 instagram.com/ellebeaumontbooks

## Standalones

Die From A Broken Heart

The Dragon's Bride

The Castle of Thorns

## Gods Among Us

Apple of Fate

## Demons of Frosteria

Frost Mate

Frost Claim (Oct '22)

## Immortal Realms Trilogy

Seeds of Sorrow (May '22)

Tides of Torment (June '23)

## Music & Wraiths

The Spirit of You

## The Hunter Series

Hunter's Truce

Royal's Vow

Assassin's Gambit

Queen's Edge

**Baron Weaver Series**

Game of Bezique

**Secrets of Galathea**

Brotherhood of the Sea

Bindings of the Sea

Voice of the Sea

King of the Sea

**Anthologies**

Of The Deep

Blood From A Stone

Cirque de vol Mystique

Link by Link

Something in the Shadows

Stories For Nerds

Emporium of Superstition (Oct '22)

**Continue reading for the first chapter of The Dragon's Bride by Christis Christie & Elle Beaumont!!**

# 1

## IMARA

With a slight press of the blade tied to her belt, the stem of the witch hazel snapped between her fingers, coming away from the body of the plant to be placed in the small pile in her lap. Overhead, the sun shone down upon her shoulders with an almost blistering heat—unobscured by even the smallest of clouds. Imara couldn't remember the last time the noonday sun had been pleasant, rather than a sweltering force to abide, the days trying to hold on to the last dregs of a fading summer as fall approached.

"Oh, this won't do," she murmured to herself, examining the sprig, then the bush as a whole.

"What was that?" came a voice from over her shoulder.

Leaning back on her heels, Imara lifted her hand to brush the back of her wrist across her forehead, ending with a swipe of her fingers through the blond strands of hair at her temple, tucking them behind one delicately pointed ear. The grass-covered roof beneath her had seen better days. Where once thick, luscious green blades had grown, now yellow spiky strands fought to stay alive.

What life was left in the soil had been driven toward the herbs and flowers Imara had planted several years ago, her father doing what he could to keep her garden alive.

"This witch hazel is dry as a bone. I don't know that I'll get much more than this harvest out of it," she stated, glancing over at her sister currently struggling to draw water from the soil around the house, sprinkling it over the rooftop garden once it had gathered upon her fingertips in small, perfectly formed spheres.

Words hardly free of Imara's lips, a spray of water splashed over her face and down the front of her. "Asta, the garden, not my face!"

Imara shot an irritated glare at her sister, who released a giggle of surprise before offering an apologetic smile.

"I'm sorry, that wasn't intentional, I promise. I wasn't paying enough attention to where I was pointing," Asta explained, reaching out to brush a few drops of water from Imara's face. Collecting them with a soft tickle of magic upon her skin, she turned to sprinkle them over the bush of witch hazel.

"Fortunately, it was rather refreshing." Imara cast an accusatory glance toward the sun. Whatever relief could be found from its rays was welcomed.

Brushing a trickle of water along her own temples, Asta turned and plopped down at the edge of the roof, her feet braced where the roof became actual ground. "When do you expect Birger today?"

Clipping one last branch from the bush, Imara turned

to sit beside Asta, her eyes drifting over their lands. Situated just a stone's throw away from the village of Omdahl, their little farm was immersed in a breathtaking landscape of rolling hills dappled with tall, branchy trees and split below by a winding river that reflected the blue skies above. The seidr had chosen this valley to settle in many moons ago due to the snow-capped mountains that loomed on either side, majestic giants of protection that graciously supplied fresh spring water to the village and its inhabitants. The valley had also been a land of opportunity, its soil rich and fertile—the perfect place for a people known to cherish the earth and all that she supplied to take root themselves.

Their family plot had been the ideal location for raising sheep and growing cotton—the supply for Dagny Hjelmstad's beautiful woven fabrics and tapestries. Erlend had seen in these fields everything he had hoped to give his new wife: the home, the opportunity, the prospering family. It was everything—until the rains stopped coming, the river began to dry up, and the soil turned to dust beneath their feet.

"He usually arrives about midday, once he has passed through Omdahl proper and spoken to anyone who has dealings with him there." Imara glanced down at the small pile of witch hazel in her lap—not nearly the offering she had hoped to have once he arrived but the best that she had to give.

Asta peered up at the sun, gauging the time by its

position in the sky. "It's half past two, but is there time for a quick drink before we need to bundle and prepare that?" she asked, eyes flicking quickly to indicate the witch hazel.

Nodding slightly, Imara pulled up the corners of the blue apron-skirt layered over her green shift, containing all of the branches she had cut, and rose to her feet. Having been outdoors for some time now, a break from the sunshine was more than warranted by both.

"Yes, let's fetch ourselves some water and perhaps run some down to Father. He's been working in the fields since early this morning." Keeping the corners of her apron-skirt swept up, Imara walked off the roof and down the small bank to the front of their home, the curved white frame set just inside the hillside as familiar to her as her own self.

Toeing the partially opened door all the way, she stepped into their home. Her mother, Dagny, stood before a loom, a finger tapping idly upon her lips as she contemplated it. Moving easily to her side, Imara pressed a soft kiss to her cheek.

"It looks beautiful, Mother, as all your pieces do. Jorunn will love it," she murmured in passing, slipping by to deposit her collection of branches onto the table.

"Thank you, Mari," was her mother's contemplative response.

Behind her, Asta came into the house with a flourish of cotton skirts and the scent of spring rain, her elemental affinity so strong she wore it like a mantle upon herself. As Imara brushed a few lost yellow petals off her skirt, her sister got busy pouring them glasses of water from the tap in the wall.

"Is Father down in the western field today?" Imara asked, reaching for the clay goblet Asta held out to her. The fresh mountain water was crisp and cold, sending a blessed chill through her body. A grateful sigh escaped her lips, shoulders relaxing as she soaked up the moment of relief.

"No, he took the sheep to the north pastures, so he ventured to the southern field instead to see how it is faring," Dagny murmured in a distant tone, her attention remaining more on the tapestry before her than on the girls.

Her questions answered, Imara finished her goblet of water and placed it on the counter beneath the tap. Freeing a water flask from the cabinet below, she worked on filling it with water, the tap squeaking softly in her grip.

"I'll take Ishka down," she said to Asta, letting her know there would be no need to walk down with her. "Should I take him a bite to eat as well?"

Her sister plucked a ripened apple from the basket on the table and brought it over to her. Once upon a time, Magnhild's apples had been so large one needed almost to hold it up with two hands to take a bite. Now, the crisp fruit nestled easily in her palm as she accepted it and slid it into the pocket looped around her belt.

"If Birger arrives before I've returned, please ask him

to wait. I will be but a moment," she asked of Asta, who nodded with understanding.

"Of course."

With a smile of thanks, Imara stepped out the door and back into the bright sunshine, the ground crunching beneath her soles with every step toward the paddock. Sensing her approach, Ishka wandered over, her snowy coat gleaming against the backdrop of hills, mountains, and sky. There was a brief moment of nuzzling as girl and horse greeted one another, and then Imara mounted the mare and they were off, down the lane leading to the cotton fields closest to the river.

Fingers twined lightly in the horse's mane, Imara started her in the right direction, then left the rest to Ishka. This trek down to the lower fields had been made so many times in days past that both horse and rider could have made it in the dead of night without even the glow of the moon to light their way. While communication with animals was not an elemental strength, nor could she have tapped into it if it were, there was an unspeakable bond between them, a way of understanding each other that had been there since Ishka had been a foal and given into Imara's care.

It was a swift, and easy ride down to the southern field. Spotting her father kneeled down with his hands in the soil, Imara slid off the horse's back. Smoothing a soft touch down the side of her neck, she praised Ishka for a job well done.

"Stay here, girl." With her parting words, Imara pulled her skirts up above her ankles to keep them from sticking to the cotton as she went by and headed down the row her father was in.

Down on one knee in the brown soil, his palms on the earth itself, Erlend Hjelmstad was muttering softly beneath his breath. While she could not make out the words, Imara instinctively knew that they were words of summoning, and her father was trying desperately to pull nutrients and life from deep within the ground and up into the topsoil their crop was planted in. Sensing her behind him, Erlend stopped. His head lifted and he gazed back at her over his shoulder, blue eyes a mirror of her own, shining with love as he took her in.

"Imara, haven't you a trader to meet with this afternoon?" he asked, running a soiled hand through short-cropped blond hair.

"It isn't quite time for that, and I thought you could do with some fresh water." Her hands were already upon the flask at her waist. Loosening it from her belt, she uncapped the top and held it out to him.

A look of gratefulness came over his features, and without further prodding, he stood, taking the water flask from her and tipping it back. As her father drank, Imara held a hand to her forehead, shielding her eyes from the sunlight so that she could survey the area around her. While the soil was meant to be brown, the cracked nature of it was worrisome. Both her mother and sister had been down here the day before, pulling what water there was left to the surface. It looked as if nothing had been done at all.

"It's not going so well, is it?" she asked, eyes returning to her father at last.

Erlend swiped a hand across his lips.

"No, it is not. I'm doing what I can, but there is simply nothing left in the ground to pull out of it." His hand motioned to the grounds around the cotton field. Just two months ago, they had borne green grasses and wildflowers; now they were withered, yellow, and barren.

"Is it even worth it anymore?" Imara questioned, taking in the sight of the cotton plants, perhaps only a third of them bearing anything worth gathering.

The decline had started gradually, beginning with hotter-than-typical days and a lack of fresh rain. With two water elementals in the family, fewer rainy days had never been an issue before. But then the grounds dried up faster than what had made sense. The grasses withered, flowers began dying, and everywhere one looked, the world was turning brown.

There had been difficult farming years in the past, but elemental abilities had always been able to combat it.

"To be honest, I'm not so certain. This won't be enough to supply what your mother needs for her fabrics . . . The yield simply isn't there this year." Erlend shook his head, his frustrations melting away into something resembling defeat.

It would have been nice to reach out a comforting hand and reassure him. However, reassurance wasn't something that Imara had to give. Not when, everywhere they looked, their neighbors were fighting the same effects. Each day seemed to bring new struggles, and with the lack of crops this harvest, people were beginning to question if they would have enough to get them through the winter, let alone hold over until next year for planting.

"Will there be enough wool to compensate?" They had not lost any numbers from the flock, the sheep hardy enough to withstand poorer grazing. Whether their coats had held up would be the next question.

"We'll see when we start sheering in a couple of weeks." The look in his eyes wasn't necessarily hopeful, which was difficult to see.

"What of our offerings for the Dragon Master? Do we need to lessen the amount we give?"

Each Fallfest, the residents of Omdahl welcomed Lord Lajos the Dragon Master to their celebrations. A powerful being who resided in the forests surrounding the mountains, he had centuries ago come to an agreement with the founding Elders of their village. At the commencement of the fall harvest, each household in Omdahl would provide a portion of their yearly produce, cattle, or craftmanship to him, and in return, he would keep the dragons in the woods from raining fire down upon them all.

It was a burden felt heavily by each citizen this year.

Erlend sighed. "We cannot, you know it. Each family offers up the same portion of their goods. We are not the only ones suffering this season. There can be no leniency for us if it is not offered also to them." His features were pinched with concern.

Imara's father had always been a lighthearted man. While he worked long, hard days to care for their crops and the flock, he had always upheld a cheerful countenance. Worry was a weighted cloak that had come only recently to rest on the Hjelmstad family's shoulders.

"Something will work out," Imara assured him, feigning confidence she did not feel. Pressing a soft kiss to his cheek, she left him to his work and returned to Ishka, who awaited her patiently.

As Imara came up the hill to the family house, she was welcomed by the sight of a small horse-drawn cart covered by a canvas tarp that hid several items beneath. It was a sight that brought a smile to her lips, and without thought, she urged Ishka on a little faster. The days of splurging were behind them, but her trade relationship with Birger was the one allowance Imara still afforded herself. It came at no cost to her family, her small rooftop garden supplying the barter items Birger required for their exchanges.

The cart's seat sat empty, his horses standing unattended and unconcerned. Releasing Ishka back into the paddock, Imara was drawn toward the open door of their home, familiar voices sounding out from its depths.

Inside she found her mother and sister seated at the table with Birger, who was in the midst of sipping tea from a clay mug. Her presence did not go unnoticed, and all three turned to look her way, greeting her with three unique smiles.

"Miss Imara!" Birger called. Setting down his tea, he held his hand out to her, which she took as she approached. The rough fingers used to holding leather reins gave hers a fond squeeze. "As always, it is a pleasure to see you. I managed to find not two but three of the volumes you were seeking."

Smiling at the warm greeting, she pulled out the wooden chair beside him and took a seat, noticing that the witch hazel she had picked this morning was neatly bundled in cheesecloth and tied with twine—Asta had been kind in her absence.

As they began to speak, her mother left the table to fill their little teapot with more water from the tap. As she turned back toward the table, her hand rested upon its ceramic side until steam rose from the white spout. A mug with tea leaves nestled in the bottom was placed before Imara, and then her mother poured in the now steaming liquid, leaving the perfect amount of room for a dollop of cream to be added once she was ready. Imara waited for the leaves to settle at the bottom, then added a tiny portion of cream from the small jug on the table. Letting it all steep for the time being, she peered over at their guest.

"That is wonderful to hear, but I don't know that what

I have is worth three hard-sought-after books on mage medicines. Try as I might, I couldn't keep the witch hazel from drying out," she explained.

"Nonsense," he replied. "Our arrangement has always been my books for one bunch of witch hazel, and that is what you've offered up."

"Yes, but—"

"Imara." He reached out to rest his hand over the top of hers on the table. "I've seen the state of Omdahl." He shook his head before continuing. "I'm not looking for more than what you are able to give right now."

# THE DRAGON'S BRIDE BY CHRISTIS CHRISTIE & ELLE BEAUMONT

**If you loved the first chapter, you can snag it On your favorite retailer!**

Available in ebook and paperback

*Vault of Glass by Candace Robinson*

**A determined girl without answers. A hot guy who would do anything for her. A mysterious museum that some see and some don't...**

Perrie Madeline lives a simple life. Her only concern is deciding whether or not to let herself fall for her hot friend, August Hartley. That is, until a strange museum known as Quinsey Wolfe's Glass Vault appears overnight and people around her begin to go missing.

Determined to uncover the Glass Vault's hidden secrets, Perrie and August conspire to break inside. But soon, Perrie realizes she has more to worry about than her feelings for August—something sinister is on their heels. Together they must find their way out of the museum before they discover something truly not for the faint of heart.

*Available Now*

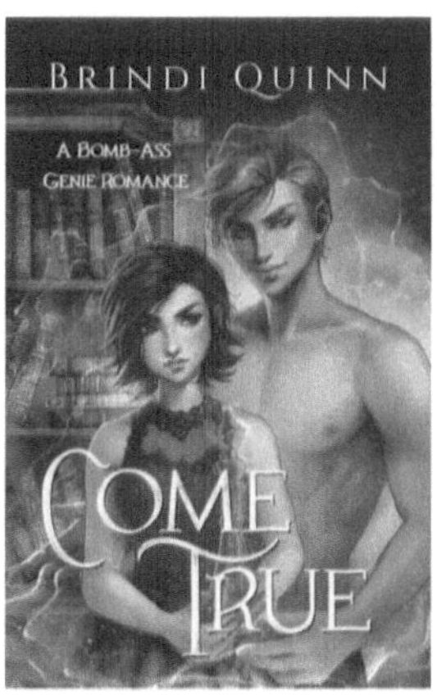

**Come True by Brindi Quinn**

A jaded girl. A persistent genie. A contest of souls.

Recent college graduate Dolly Jones has spent the last year stubbornly trying to atone for a mistake that cost her everything. She doesn't go out, she doesn't make new friends and she sure as hell doesn't treat herself to things she hasn't earned, but when her most recent thrift store purchase proves home to a hot, magical genie determined to draw out her darkest desires in exchange for a taste of her soul, Dolly's restraint, and patience, will be put to the test.

Newbie genie Velis Reilhander will do anything to beat his older half-brothers in a soul-collecting contest that will determine the next heir to their family estate, even if it means coaxing desire out of the least palatable human he's ever contracted. As a djinn from a 'polluted' bloodline, Velis knows what it's like to work twice as hard as everyone else, and he won't let anyone—not even Dolly f*cking Jones—stand in the way of his birthright. He just needs to

figure out her heart's greatest desire before his asshole brothers
can get to her first.

Available 4.27.22